The Three Musketeers

Artists: Penko Gelev
Sotir Gelev

First edition for North America (including Canada and Mexico), Philippine Islands, and Puerto Rico published in 2008 by Barron's Educational Series, Inc.

All inquiries should be addressed to:
Barron's Educational Series, Inc.
250 Wireless Boulevard
Hauppauge, New York 11788
www.barronseduc.com

ISBN-13 (Hardcover): 978-0-7641-6056-1
ISBN-10 (Hardcover): 0-7641-6056-7

ISBN-13 (Paperback): 978-0-7641-3780-8
ISBN-10 (Paperback): 0-7641-3780-8

Library of Congress Control No.: 2008923569

Picture credits:
p. 40 World History Archive/Topfoto
p. 43 Roger-Viollet/Topfoto
p. 45 Carolyn Franklin
p. 47 TopFoto/HIP/Photographer: Mike Newell
Every effort has been made to trace copyright holders. The Salariya Book Company apologizes for any omissions and would be pleased, in such cases, to add an acknowledgment in future editions.

Printed and bound in China
9 8 7 6 5 4 3 2 1

The Three Musketeers

Alexandre Dumas

ILLUSTRATED BY
Penko Gelev

RETOLD BY
Jim Pipe

SERIES CREATED AND DESIGNED BY
David Salariya

At two o'clock in the morning our four adventurers left Paris. As long as it was dark, they kept silent; in spite of themselves, they were affected by the darkness and saw ambushes everywhere.

At the first glimmer of daybreak, their tongues were untied. With the sun, their gaiety returned. Just as on the day before a battle, their hearts thumped, their eyes laughed, and they felt that the life which they might be about to lose was, on the whole, a good thing.

(see page 18)

CHARACTERS

D'Artagnan

Aramis

Porthos

Athos

The Three Musketeers

King Louis XIII

Queen Anne

Cardinal Richelieu

Milady de Winter

Monsieur de Tréville

The Duke of Buckingham

Lord de Winter

John Felton

Constance Bonacieux

Monsieur Bonacieux

Madame de Chevreuse

Planchet
D'Artagnan's servant

Grimaud
Athos' servant

Bazin
Aramis' servant

Mousqueton
Porthos' servant

D'Artagnan Leaves Home

April 1625

> Go and see M.[1] de Tréville with this letter.

> Take care of yourself!

D'Artagnan, a young man from Gascony,[2] is leaving home to make his fortune in Paris. To help him on his way, his father gives him his old yellow horse, a small sum of money, and a letter of introduction.

D'Artagnan's father tells him to take orders from no one but the King, the Cardinal, and M. de Tréville. His mother gives him a herbal medicine that heals any wound.

> What are you laughing at?

> Your horse is as yellow as a buttercup!

> A plague on these Gascons!

> What are your plans?

> I'm returning to Paris, Milady.[3]

In the town of Meung, a group of strangers laugh at his old horse. Furious, D'Artagnan picks a fight with their leader, a nobleman.

D'Artagnan is attacked by the nobleman's thugs. Raining blows on him with sticks and shovels, they knock him out.

When he comes to, D'Artagnan sees the nobleman talking to a woman in a coach. He cannot help noticing her long, curly hair and sparkling blue eyes.

> Come back, you coward!

> I'd rather lose a thousand pistoles[4] than that letter!

D'Artagnan runs out, ready for another fight, but the nobleman leaps on his horse and gallops away. The coach also speeds off.

Still weak from his injuries, D'Artagnan collapses in the road.

Just as he is about to leave town himself, D'Artagnan discovers that the gentleman has stolen his letter to M. de Tréville!

1. M.: short for Monsieur, which is French for "Mister."
2. Gascony: a province in southwest France. People from Gascony are called Gascons.
3. Milady: an old-fashioned pronunciation of the English title "My Lady."
4. pistole: a gold coin worth about ten livres or francs in old French money.

THE MUSKETEERS

The young Gascon doggedly rides on to Paris. He sells his horse and enters the city on foot, seeking out the home of M. de Tréville, captain of the King's Musketeers.

The courtyard of M. de Tréville's house

D'Artagnan admires the musketeers' swordplay and tales of war. On the stairway he passes four musketeers fencing and laughing like fools.

The Cardinal has bandy legs!

His girlfriend must like them!

Later, as he waits to see the Captain, D'Artagnan hears them mocking Cardinal Richelieu, the most powerful man in France.

Porthos, Aramis, what were you up to?

The Captain calls two of the men inside. He scolds them for fighting the Cardinal's guards.

I see—so the Cardinal was exaggerating.

They attacked us before we could draw our swords.

What does this have to do with me?

Porthos and Aramis reply that the Cardinal's men ambushed them, wounding their friend Athos and killing two others.

The musketeers fought back, killing a couple of the Cardinal's men before being arrested. Later, they managed to escape.

Just then, a third musketeer, Athos, staggers into the room. He is clearly in great pain from his wound. With a loud groan, he collapses onto the floor.

While Athos is being treated, D'Artagnan finally speaks to Captain de Tréville. He asks to join the King's Musketeers.

D'Artagnan tells his story. The Captain is all ears when he hears about the mysterious nobleman and Milady.

The Captain then asks D'Artagnan what he thinks of the Cardinal. He suspects the young man may be a spy.

Satisfied with D'Artagnan's answer, de Tréville invites him to join the musketeers as a cadet.[1] But just then, D'Artagnan dashes from the room—he has spotted the mysterious nobleman from Meung!

D'Artagnan runs straight into Athos, who howls in pain from his wound. Athos is hopping mad and challenges D'Artagnan to a duel at noon that day.

Rushing off, D'Artagnan tries to slip between two men but gets caught up in a cloak. It belongs to the giant Porthos, who challenges him to a duel at one o'clock.

1. cadet: a trainee officer.

A Duel Becomes A Fight

You'd be sorry to lose this!

I think you're mistaken; it isn't mine.

I won't survive three duels in a row, but at least I'll die at the hands of a famous musketeer.

Still looking for the man from Meung, D'Artagnan sees Aramis. He helpfully picks up a handkerchief that Aramis is trying to hide under his foot.

The handkerchief belongs to Aramis' secret love. Furious that his secret is out, Aramis challenges D'Artagnan to a duel at two o'clock.

My shoulder's on fire!

Take this. I'll fight you when you're healed.

I'm fighting him at one!

Me too, at two!

Do you do everything together?

Put up your swords!

D'Artagnan offers to heal Athos with his mother's balm.[1] But Athos wants to get on with the duel.

Aramis and Porthos arrive soon after to witness the duel. The three musketeers are embarrassed that they are all fighting the same young man.

D'Artagnan and Athos have just drawn their swords when the Cardinal's guards appear. They try to arrest the musketeers for dueling.

No, we are four— my heart is a musketeer's!

They are five; we are just three.

The nine men rush at each other in a great fury. The fight is on!

Aramis mocks Jussac, the leader of the Cardinal's guards. When Jussac's men get ready to attack, D'Artagnan decides to fight alongside the three musketeers.

1. balm: a healing or soothing medicine.

D'Artagnan slips under Jussac's blade and runs him through…

…then rescues Athos in the nick of time.

The other guards surrender and the musketeers take their swords. Linking arms, they return to the Captain's house in triumph.

Have them come tomorrow—by the back stairs.

King Louis XIII hears about the fight from the Captain. He wants to meet the four heroes.

The musketeers arrive early. They ask their new friend D'Artagnan to play tennis with them, but he is no match for the others.

Are you afraid of the ball?

One of the Cardinal's finest swordsmen, Bernajoux, is watching the game. Looking for revenge, he jeers at D'Artagnan.

On guard!

Hurry up, I've got an appointment at noon!

D'Artagnan's blood boils. He challenges Bernajoux to a duel.

Take that!

When Bernajoux is wounded, his friends attack D'Artagnan. Then the three musketeers join in. But in the middle of the fight, D'Artagnan remembers their meeting with the King!

A KIDNAPPING

D'Artagnan's duel with Bernajoux is the talk of the town, but the musketeers are cleared of any blame. When they meet the King in the Louvre palace, he thanks them and gives D'Artagnan a fistful of gold.

The musketeers are thrilled. So is the King, who looks forward to teasing Richelieu. The Cardinal is so angry that he avoids the King for a week.

Over the next few weeks, the three musketeers and D'Artagnan become firm friends, spending all their time together. Porthos helps D'Artagnan to hire a servant named Planchet.

One day, a stranger comes knocking on D'Artagnan's door. It is his landlord, M. Bonacieux. His wife, who works for the Queen, has been kidnapped!

Bonacieux believes the kidnap is linked to a love affair between the Queen and the English Duke of Buckingham. D'Artagnan agrees to help. The kidnapper sounds like the man from Meung. Just then, D'Artagnan spots him across the street.

1. Santé: French for "Cheers," or "Good health."

D'Artagnan is off like a shot, just as Porthos, Athos, and Aramis arrive.

He's vanished like a ghost!

Once again, D'Artagnan loses sight of his quarry. Returning to his rooms, he asks his three friends for advice.

We must help, if only to stop the Cardinal!

They suspect the kidnap has been organized by the Cardinal, who hates the Queen. The four friends agree to help Mme.[1] Bonacieux and the Queen.

In the name of Heaven, save me!

All of a sudden, the door opens with a loud bang. Bonacieux rushes in. He begs D'Artagnan to rescue him from the Cardinal's guards, who have come to arrest him.

Go on, gentlemen, take this knave away!

Strangely, D'Artagnan does not stop the Cardinal's men from arresting Bonacieux. In fact, he pushes the landlord into their arms and even praises the Cardinal.

Porthos, you twit, D'Artagnan did exactly the right thing!

Porthos is confused, but Aramis explains that D'Artagnan was right; they cannot take any risks until they know what is going on. The four friends then swear to support each other through thick and thin.

ALL FOR ONE AND ONE FOR ALL!

1. Mme.: short for Madame, which is French for "Mrs."

D'Artagnan Falls in Love

They've set a trap!

The Cardinal's men arrest all visitors to Bonacieux's rooms and question them. D'Artagnan listens through a hole in the floor.

When Mme. Bonacieux appears, the guards try to bind and gag her.

D'Artagnan bursts in…

…and it doesn't take long…

…to clear the room!

Monsieur, Thank you for saving me!

They arrested your husband. We should leave now.

We must warn the Queen.

Athos is out, but you'll be safe here.

He will think I was here when I was really fighting the guards.

Mme. Bonacieux explains how she escaped from her kidnappers: she lowered herself from a window using sheets. D'Artagnan decides she will be safer at Athos' house.

There, Mme. Bonacieux begs D'Artagnan to warn the Queen. Using secret passwords to enter the Louvre palace, he meets with Germain, the Queen's loyal valet.[1]

D'Artagnan visits M. de Tréville to give himself an alibi.[2] When the Captain looks away, he changes the clock!

1. valet: a personal servant, usually a man.
2. alibi: a defense used by an accused person to prove they were somewhere else when a crime took place.

She's so pretty... and I'm so poor!

Pardieu,[1] what is she doing here at this time?

D'Artagnan has fallen madly in love with Constance Bonacieux. He wanders the streets, dreaming of her.

He goes to ask Aramis for advice. But he is surprised to see a woman tapping on his friend's door. When the door opens, he sees not Aramis, but another woman.

The two women say nothing. They swap handkerchiefs, and the visitor leaves. D'Artagnan gasps when he sees her face—it's Constance Bonacieux!

You were at my friend Aramis' house.

Why are you following me?

Aramis? Who is that?

You're so mysterious...

Does that bother you?

D'Artagnan chases after Mme. Bonacieux and stops her. She is shocked to see him, but is also touched that he is so concerned about her.

Mme. Bonacieux allows D'Artagnan to escort her to another house on her secret mission—but first he must promise not to spy on her again.

When they found Athos in your rooms, they mistook him for you.

She swore she did not know Aramis!

A thousand pardons, Milord;[2] I was jealous.

When D'Artagnan returns home, his servant Planchet tells him the Cardinal's men have arrested Athos.

D'Artagnan returns to the Louvre to talk to the Captain. He spots Mme. Bonacieux again—this time being escorted by Aramis! In a jealous rage, he confronts them.

But the man is not Aramis—it's the Duke of Buckingham, on his way to a secret meeting with the Queen. Embarrassed, D'Artagnan offers to escort them to the palace.

1. Pardieu: Oh my God!
2. Milord: My lord.

THE CARDINAL'S TRAP

Inside the Louvre palace

We must not meet again.

I know—I'm a fool for ever thinking we could be together.

The Duke of Buckingham meets secretly with Queen Anne.

I have walked into the Cardinal's trap: it may cost me my life!

Go away, I beg you! It's too dangerous.

The Duke is head over heels in love; he cannot stay away. He is even ready to start a war between England and France, just so that he can be near the Queen when the peace treaty is agreed.

I'll go if you give me a token of your love.

Then keep this in memory of me.

The Queen gives the Duke a diamond necklace, which was a birthday present from the King. Then Mme. Bonacieux sneaks the Duke out of the palace.

Meanwhile...

You are accused of treason![1]

Have mercy on me!

...in the dreaded Bastille prison

M. Bonacieux is being grilled by Cardinal Richelieu. Terrified, he repeats every word his wife has told him about the Queen and the Duke of Buckingham.

Nothing is hidden from me, nothing!

The Cardinal persuades M. Bonacieux to spy on his wife, in return for his freedom and 100 pistoles.

Give this letter to Milady! Later...

The Queen must not realize her secret is out!

Thanks to his spies, the Cardinal finds out about the Queen's gift to the Duke. He sends a letter to his agent known as Milady, ordering her to steal two diamond pendants[2] from the necklace.

Next day...

Captain de Tréville hears that Athos has been arrested. He goes straight to the King. He can prove that Athos was dining with two noblemen when the Cardinal's men were attacked.

1. treason: plotting against the king or government; betraying one's country.
2. pendants: hanging ornaments.

M. de Tréville also provides an alibi for D'Artagnan—not knowing that D'Artagnan turned back the clock. The King agrees to free Athos. The Captain leaves, but suspects the Cardinal is up to no good!

The Cardinal tells the King of the Duke's visit to Paris. He pretends to defend the Queen, but hints at a plot between her, the Duke, and France's enemies.

The King suspects the Queen of betraying him, and orders her rooms to be searched. The Queen is furious, but she is forced to hand over a letter hidden in her dress.

The letter reveals that the Queen is part of a plot against the Cardinal—but nothing links her to the Duke. The King feels ashamed that he did not trust her.

Slyly, the Cardinal suggests that the Queen should wear her diamond necklace to the ball. He knows full well that she has given it to the Duke. When the Queen hears this, she is horrified!

A Secret Mission to England

Mme. Bonacieux knows of a way to get the necklace back from the Duke in England. The Queen writes a letter to warn him of the Cardinal's plot.

Mme. Bonacieux asks her husband to carry the letter to the Duke. But instead of helping her, he goes off to warn the Cardinal about the Queen's letter!

Soon after, D'Artagnan knocks on Mme. Bonacieux's door; he has been listening to every word. He persuades her to let him deliver the letter to the Duke.

She gives him the money given to her husband by the Cardinal. Just then, Bonacieux returns—with the man from Meung!

D'Artagnan and Mme. Bonacieux hide in his rooms upstairs. They hear the man from Meung telling Bonacieux to steal the letter to the Duke.

D'Artagnan goes to M. de Tréville. Hearing that the Queen is in danger, the Captain agrees to let D'Artagnan go, along with Porthos, Aramis, and Athos.

That night, the four friends leave Paris.

At the first inn they stop at, a stranger picks a fight with Porthos. The others decide to keep going; Porthos can catch up later.

Two hours later, they are caught in an ambush. Aramis is shot in the shoulder and cannot ride any further.

Athos, D'Artagnan, and their two servants spend the night at an inn. They are about to leave in the morning when four of the Cardinal's men burst in. Athos holds them off while D'Artagnan and his servant Planchet make their escape.

D'Artagnan travels on to England. He finds the Duke of Buckingham at Windsor and hands him the Queen's letter.

The Duke takes out the necklace and gasps: it is missing two pendants! He sends an order blocking French ships from leaving England. The thief must not reach France until the pendants have been replaced.

As soon as the necklace is repaired, D'Artagnan races back to France with it.

A Secret Rendezvous

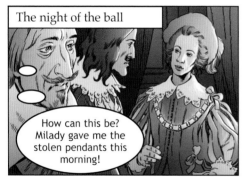

The night of the ball

How can this be? Milady gave me the stolen pendants this morning!

The Cardinal gives the King the pendants stolen by Milady, hoping the Queen will be forced to admit her secret meetings with the Duke. But, thanks to D'Artagnan, the necklace she wears is complete!

The King is pleased to see the Queen wearing his necklace. The Queen is even more delighted with her victory over the Cardinal.

Later that night…

D'Artagnan is invited to the Queen's rooms. A hand appears from behind a tapestry. Realizing it belongs to the Queen, D'Artagnan falls to his knees and kisses it.

She gives D'Artagnan a diamond ring—a reward for saving her from the Cardinal and Milady de Winter.

Be still, my beating heart!

When D'Artagnan returns to his rooms, Planchet hands him a letter from Constance inviting him to a secret rendezvous[1] the following night.

The next morning…

That ring will betray the man who wears it.

I'll never sell it!

M. de Tréville warns D'Artagnan to sell the ring before anyone guesses where it came from.

That night, D'Artagnan and Planchet set off for the rendezvous, both heavily armed.

Did she fall asleep waiting for me?

D'Artagnan waits for Constance at the agreed place. After an hour, he starts to worry. He claps his hands three times, but there is no reply.

What should I do?

In the name of Heaven, what did you see?

Find your three friends. On your return I may have more news.

Climbing a tree, D'Artagnan peeps into an upstairs window, hoping to see Constance. Instead, he sees there has been a violent struggle!

D'Artagnan hammers on the door. Finally, a scared old man appears. He tells how a group of three men kidnapped Constance. A short, fat man pointed her out to them.

D'Artagnan goes to see M. de Tréville. The Captain suspects the Cardinal has been up to his old tricks.

Later…

Hmm… short and fat, like the man who helped the kidnappers!

The next day…

I twisted my knee in that duel. I'll be fine in a few days.

What happened to you?

D'Artagnan bumps into Bonacieux. Was he involved in the kidnap?

D'Artagnan tracks down Porthos. Finding him alive and well, he travels on to the inn where he left the wounded Aramis.

To his surprise, D'Artagnan finds Aramis and two priests discussing religion. Aramis has decided to become a priest!

She slipped, and I saw the fleur-de-lis[2] on her shoulder. My angel was a demon!

It's me, your friend D'Artagnan.

But when D'Artagnan hands Aramis a letter from his girlfriend, he changes his mind.[1]

At the next inn, D'Artagnan finds that Athos and his servant Grimaud have locked themselves in the wine cellar. He persuades them to come out.

A drunken Athos confesses a terrible secret to D'Artagnan: he was once married, but threw his wife out of the house when he found out she was a criminal.

1. he changes his mind: because priests are not allowed to have girlfriends.
2. fleur-de-lis: a French lily, a flower used as a symbol by French kings. It was also branded onto thieves using a red-hot iron.

A Duel with Lord de Winter

Back in Paris...

Congratulations, D'Artagnan!

But where will I get the money to pay for my outfit?

A message comes from M. de Tréville. War has broken out with England: the musketeers have two weeks to buy new equipment. D'Artagnan has been asked to join the King's Guards as a cadet. But he is too worried about Constance to enjoy the good news.

A few days later...

By chance, D'Artagnan spies Milady de Winter in church. He follows her. Can she help him find Constance?

As Milady gets into her carriage, a stranger rides up. They begin to argue in English.

Mind your own business, featherbrain!

When D'Artagnan steps in, Milady tells him that the man is her brother-in-law, Lord de Winter. She drives off in a huff. Lord de Winter is about to follow when D'Artagnan grabs his horse's bridle.[1]

You can see I have no sword.

Then find your longest and bring it along this evening!

Lord de Winter is furious and insults D'Artagnan. Hot-tempered as ever, D'Artagnan challenges him to a duel.

That evening...

Gentlemen, are we ready?

D'Artagnan meets Lord de Winter, taking Porthos, Aramis, and Athos to act as witnesses to the duel.

1. bridle: the harness that fits over a horse's head, used to control the horse.

All four friends get drawn into a fast, furious fight. Athos stabs his man through the heart. Aramis and Porthos soon defeat their opponents.

I'll let you live—out of love for your sister-in-law.

Then I must invite you to meet her.

I just want to find out if Milady is behind the kidnapping.

Watch out—it could be a trap!

The next day…

Thank you for sparing my brother's life.

D'Artagnan spares Lord de Winter.

Athos is confused: isn't D'Artagnan in love with Constance? D'Artagnan explains his plan.

Lord de Winter introduces D'Artagnan to Milady. She is very charming, but D'Artagnan can see she is secretly furious with her brother-in-law.

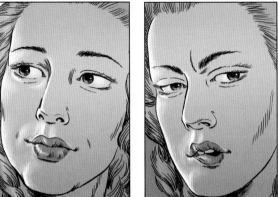

D'Artagnan sees Milady's face in the mirror when she thinks no one is looking. His blood runs cold as her sweet smile turns to a murderous scowl.

But D'Artagnan is also being watched—Milady's maid Kitty has her eye on the dashing young guardsman!

23

MILADY'S TERRIBLE SECRET

I'll do anything for you!

Will you help me against your mistress?

Suddenly...

I can hear Milady coming. Quick—hide in my room!

Over the next few days, D'Artagnan continues to visit Milady. He hopes to find out where Constance has been taken.

Kitty tells D'Artagnan that Milady is in love with the Count de Wardes—and Kitty herself has fallen in love with D'Artagnan!

The idiot should have killed Lord de Winter when he had the chance!

That woman is a monster!

Hateful creature!

Sssssh— she'll hear you!

That's enough talk. You can go now, Kitty.

D'Artagnan overhears Milady telling Kitty that he is a fool. She would have killed him already if the Cardinal hadn't told her to spare him.

Milady also mentions her role in Constance's kidnapping. So she *is* the Cardinal's agent! D'Artagnan boils with rage, but Kitty warns him to be quiet.

Tell Milady the Count de Wardes will pay her a visit tonight.

Keep this ring as a sign of my love.

D'Artagnan asks Kitty to show him the letters between Milady and her admirer Count de Wardes. He has a plan…

D'Artagnan disguises himself as the Count and creeps into Milady's room at night from Kitty's room next door. The room is very dark and Milady is fooled by the disguise.

Milady gives D'Artagnan a ring, still thinking he is the Count de Wardes. He leaves while it is still dark.

The next day…

Can I rely on you?

Pretending to be the
Count de Wardes,
D'Artagnan writes to
Milady that he cannot
see her again.

Milady flies into a rage and
swears revenge on the Count.
She invites D'Artagnan to come
and see her, then asks him to kill
the Count for her!

It wasn't the
Count who came
to see you—it
was me!

D'Artagnan shows Milady the
ring, revealing the trick he has
played on her.

In the struggle, her dress
tears—and he sees a fleur-de-lis
burnt into her shoulder!

Good God!
You're a branded
criminal!

Now you know
my secret, you
must die!

Milady pulls out a dagger and
lunges at D'Artagnan.

Disguised in Kitty's
clothes, D'Artagnan
slips out of the house.

You vile
beast!

Milady hurls herself at
D'Artagnan but he leaps out of
the way. Escaping into Kitty's
room, he bolts the door.

In frustration, Milady flings
herself against the heavy door,
stabbing it with the dagger
and screaming wildly.

25

THE CARDINAL'S OFFER

D'Artagnan dashes to Athos' home and tells him everything. They suspect Milady de Winter is none other than Athos' wife.

The two of them return to D'Artagnan's rooms. Kitty is waiting for them, terrified that Milady will punish her.

Bonacieux is in the doorway. Kitty is afraid he will recognize her. She suspects he is Milady's spy.

Soon after, Aramis pays a visit. He has found a job for Kitty outside Paris, where she will be safe from Milady.

D'Artagnan and Athos sell Milady's sapphire ring to buy weapons, horses, and uniforms.

D'Artagnan finds two letters waiting for him. One is from Constance, asking him to meet her that night. The other is an order to meet the Cardinal.

As D'Artagnan waits alone, a carriage races by.

From the window, Constance blows him a kiss. Is she safe, or is she a prisoner of the Cardinal?

Beware—you have powerful enemies.

D'Artagnan's meeting with the Cardinal is equally mysterious. The Cardinal hints that he knows what D'Artagnan has been doing. Strangely, he doesn't seem angry.

If you refuse me, I can no longer protect you!

He offers D'Artagnan a job as an officer in his own Guards. Amazed, D'Artagnan politely turns down the offer.

Two days later, D'Artagnan leaves Paris with the King's Guards. The Musketeers will follow later.

The guards ride to La Rochelle, a town captured by the English and now besieged[1] by the French.

It's an ambush!

Should I thank Milady or the Cardinal for this?

One evening, as D'Artagnan goes for a leisurely stroll, he sees the gleam of a musket barrel in the setting sun. What danger lurks behind that hedge?

D'Artagnan throws himself to the ground, just as a bullet whizzes over his head. Leaping up, he runs as fast as his legs can carry him. A second shot knocks his hat off, but he scrambles to safety.

1. besieged: surrounded by soldiers so that the defenders cannot get out or bring in food and supplies from outside.

MILADY'S REVENGE

The next day, D'Artagnan volunteers to lead a dangerous mission close to the city walls. The two men who attacked him the night before also volunteer.

D'Artagnan's party soon comes under fire.

Suddenly, more shots are fired at them from behind!

Let's finish him off!

It's the two assassins from yesterday! D'Artagnan falls to the ground, pretending to be hit. Thinking he is wounded, the assassins come closer.

Suddenly, D'Artagnan leaps up and kills one of the assassins.

Don't kill me! I'll tell you everything.

He quickly overpowers the second one and threatens to kill him if he doesn't talk.

So Constance was escaping when I saw her!

The assassins have a letter from Milady. It reveals that Constance is now hiding safely in a convent.

A few days later...

D'Artagnan receives a dozen bottles of fine wine—a gift from his friends, the musketeers.

Who should I thank for the wine?

Not me!

Or me!

He is just about to enjoy a glass of the wine when Aramis, Porthos, and Athos arrive in the camp. They all say that they didn't send the wine. So who did?

Just then, a servant who has already tasted the wine collapses to the floor. He begins to roll around in agony. The wine is poisoned! D'Artagnan realizes he has had a narrow escape.

The friends agree to rescue Constance from the convent after the siege. Athos is secretly determined to confront Milady and stop the attacks on D'Artagnan.

One dark night soon after, the three musketeers bump into the Cardinal. They agree to act as his guards for the evening.

The musketeers follow the Cardinal to a secret meeting at the Red Dovecote Inn. While they wait downstairs in the kitchen, Athos listens through the stovepipe…

The Cardinal orders Milady to England. She must persuade Buckingham to stop the war—or the Cardinal will tell King Louis about his affair with the Queen.

In return, Milady asks the Cardinal to throw D'Artagnan in prison and to find out where Constance is hiding.

The Cardinal agrees to Milady's request. Downstairs, Athos has heard enough. He asks Aramis and Porthos to keep listening while he leaves the building.

SAINT GERVAIS FORT

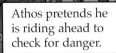

Athos pretends he is riding ahead to check for danger.

Soon after, the Cardinal sets off with Porthos and Aramis back to the army camp. Athos, who has been hiding in the trees, doubles back to the inn to confront Milady.

GASP!

Remember me?

Give me the letter or I'll blow your brains out.

Take it and be cursed!

When she recognizes him, Milady is terrified—she thought Athos, her former husband, was dead. Athos laughs at the fact that each of them thought the other was dead.

Athos warns Milady that if anything happens to D'Artagnan, he will kill her. Pointing his pistol at her head, he takes the letter the Cardinal has given her. It gives her permission to do whatever she likes—even murder!

I'll get my revenge!

Athos is going to get us killed!

Bravo! We accept the bet!

Meanwhile…

Milady travels all night. By 7 o'clock the next morning she is aboard ship. Two hours later, the ship sets sail for England.

The four friends meet at an inn for breakfast, but it is too busy for them to make any secret plans. Athos makes a bet: if the four of them can hold the nearby Saint Gervais Fort for a full hour, the other soldiers must buy them dinner.

Athos' servant Grimaud packs a lunch basket, then the four friends march up to the deserted fort. Athos explains that this is the perfect place to make plans without being overheard by the Cardinal's men.

At the fort, the men dive into their breakfast.

Their breakfast is interrupted when a party of citizens from La Rochelle attacks the fort. Soon a fierce battle rages.

As they defend the shattered walls, the musketeers discuss how to keep themselves and Buckingham safe from Milady and the Cardinal.

Grimaud hoists a napkin on top of a pike to show the other French soldiers that they have occupied the fort.

The friends decide that Aramis will write two letters. One will warn Lord de Winter, urging him to imprison Milady before she gets a chance to kill Buckingham. The other letter is to be sent to Aramis' ladyfriend, Mme. de Chevreuse, to warn the Queen of the plot against Buckingham.

MILADY'S ARREST

Is that all of them?

No, but we've been here an hour—we won the bet!

BRAVO!

Long live the brave musketeers!

The friends hold the fort for a full hour and a half, fighting off two groups of attackers. The whole French camp has been watching. When D'Artagnan and the musketeers return to camp, they are welcomed as heroes.

What's going on?

Those four men held the fort for two hours on their own.

When the next wave of attackers reaches the base of the fort, the four friends push at a section of the damaged wall. Breaking loose, it falls to the ground, crushing the attackers below.

The Cardinal hears of their bravery. Still hoping to win them over, he orders M. de Tréville to promote D'Artagnan to the Musketeers so he can be with his friends. D'Artagnan is thrilled.

How dare you keep me here!

You married my elder brother when you were already married to Athos!

Two days later…

D'Artagnan sells the Queen's ring to buy his musketeer uniform and to pay for the letters to be carried to Lord de Winter and the Queen.

When Milady arrives in England, she is arrested and taken to Lord de Winter's castle. He has read the letter from Aramis: he knows all about her criminal past, her work for the Cardinal, and the plan to assassinate Buckingham.

AAARRRGGH!

Roar all you like, but beware: I will defend myself!

Milady screams in fury but Lord de Winter continues, telling her that in two weeks she will be imprisoned on a remote island on the far side of the world.

For now, you will stay in this castle. There is no way out!

We'll see about that!

Lord de Winter then introduces Milady to her stony-faced jailer, John Felton. De Winter warns Milady that if she tries to escape, his men have been ordered to shoot her.

Is she dead? Or has she betrayed me?

Back in France…

Are you hatching a plan?

Only against the people of La Rochelle!

The siege continues, as the Cardinal waits impatiently for news from Milady. The Duke of Buckingham has sent a fleet of ships to support the rebels in La Rochelle.

Deep in thought, the Cardinal takes a walk along the beach. He spies the musketeers in the sand dunes, reading a letter. Though he tries to sneak up on them, Athos refuses to let him see the letter.

I want these four on my side!

Athos politely makes fun of the Cardinal. The Cardinal heads off with a smile on his face—but with anger burning in his heart.

As soon as the siege is over, we must rescue her.

Agreed!

The letter is from Aramis' old friend Mme. de Chevreuse, who has found out that Constance is being kept in a convent in the small town of Béthune.

THE ESCAPE

Back in England, Milady furiously plots her escape. She dreams of getting even with D'Artagnan.

Milady pretends to faint to gain the sympathy of her jailer, John Felton. When this fails, she fakes an illness.

Milady then lies to Felton: she says that Buckingham branded her with the fleur-de-lis after she refused to become his lover.

She claims that Buckingham murdered her husband, Lord de Winter's brother. She fled to France, but when she returned, Buckingham forced de Winter to arrest her.

When Lord de Winter enters the room, Milady pretends to stab herself—though she is protected by a metal strap under her clothing. Felton now believes Milady's story; what's more, he has fallen in love with her.

Lord de Winter sends Felton away because he suspects Milady has won him over. Milady almost gives up hope. But on a dark and stormy night, the day before she is to be taken away, Felton appears at her window—with a file and a rope ladder!

As soon as he has cut the iron bars, Milady climbs out of the window.

They both hold their breath as the guards walk past below.

Finally they reach safety. Felton carries Milady down to the beach and they escape in a small boat.

Don't worry—I'll deal with Buckingham.

The fool! He believed all my lies!

Together they sail to Portsmouth,[1] where Buckingham is preparing a fleet to set out for La Rochelle.

I come from Lord de Winter.

Pretending to have an urgent message for the Duke, Felton is allowed to see Buckingham.

Let her go!

Never!

At first, Felton tries to persuade Buckingham to free Milady. When he refuses, Felton pulls out a dagger and stabs Buckingham through the heart.

I knew it—I'm too late!

Felton tries to escape but is arrested on the stairs by Lord de Winter and his men.

The Queen says she has always loved you.

As Buckingham lies dying, a messenger arrives with a letter from Queen Anne, begging him to stop the war against France.

The Duke dies a happy man. As Felton is dragged away, he sees Milady's ship on the horizon. She has escaped without him!

---

1. Portsmouth: the most important naval base in England, on the south coast.

CONSTANCE IN DANGER!

Back in France…

The musketeers have heard that Milady is heading for the convent where Constance is hiding. They ask M. de Tréville for four days' leave.

But Milady reaches the convent first…

I know all about your kidnapping.

So you know how I've suffered!

Pretending to be an old friend of D'Artagnan, Milady quickly gains Constance's trust. Constance confesses her love for D'Artagnan.

Now I can get even with D'Artagnan!

Constance shows Milady a letter saying that D'Artagnan is coming to rescue her. Milady can't believe her luck.

They hear a horse approaching.

Is that D'Artagnan already?

But instead of D'Artagnan, it is the Count de Rochefort, the Cardinal's spy—the man from Meung!

The Cardinal sent me to look for you.

Milady asks him to send a carriage to take her and Constance to Armentières. He doesn't know the place, so she writes the name down for him.

Let's get him!

No, let him go— he's heading the other way.

He gallops past an inn where the musketeers have stopped. Aramis persuades D'Artagnan to let him go. However, as Rochefort gallops away, the note from Milady falls out of his hat.

It just says the name of a town: Armentières.

Alerted by the sight of Rochefort, the four musketeers gallop with even greater speed to the convent.

I'm too weak to go—save yourself!

I've got a better idea!

Drink this wine, it'll give you strength.

This is not the revenge I planned, but it will do!

Hearing the musketeers' horses, Milady tells Constance that the Cardinal's men have come for her. Constance is frozen in fear.

Milady pours poison from her ring into a glass of wine.

Still shaking with fear, Constance drinks the wine. Milady rushes from the apartment, but Constance is too weak to follow.

My beloved D'Artagnan, you've finally come!

Constance, Constance!

There is no antidote[1] to that poison.

D'Artagnan bursts into the room, but he is too late. The poison is already doing its deadly work.

The musketeers realize what has happened. They can do nothing as Constance dies in D'Artagnan's loving arms.

I believe we are hunting the same woman—Milady.

Yes—and she is my wife!

Milady won't know you. Let me know when you find her.

Just then, Lord de Winter himself arrives from England, in hot pursuit of Milady. Set on revenge, Athos finally reveals his big secret—he is Milady's first husband! The men agree to go to Constance's funeral before dealing with the murderous Milady.

Meanwhile, the servants Planchet, Grimaud, Bazin, and Mousqueton are sent to track down Milady in Armentières—thanks to the note dropped by the Count de Rochefort.

1. antidote: a remedy that stops or controls a poison.

DEATH OF A DEMON

The servants find Milady at the inn in Armentières. At this news, Athos heads off to fetch the final member of their party. He returns with a mysterious stranger: a man in a red cloak whose face is masked. Together they set off after Milady.

They find Milady just about to cross the border into Flanders.[1] She is alone.

The musketeers list Milady's crimes. D'Artagnan charges her with the murder of Constance, and her attempts to kill him. Lord de Winter accuses her of murdering his brother and Buckingham.

When Athos mentions the fleur-de-lis, Milady dares him to prove that she really is his wife. It is time for the stranger in the red cloak to introduce himself.

Milady falls to the ground, sobbing.

The stranger used to be the public executioner of the town of Lille. He tells how he branded Milady as a young woman for stealing and for driving a young priest to kill himself. Milady finally accepts her fate and walks outside, followed by the others.

1. Flanders: roughly equal to present-day Belgium.

The servants drag Milady to the river bank, where the executioner binds her hands and feet.

The executioner ferries Milady across the river. Athos shows no mercy, but D'Artagnan still feels sorry for Milady.

Milady slips to her knees on the muddy ground. The executioner raises his broadsword in both hands and, with a single blow, chops off her head.

When the musketeers return to La Rochelle, D'Artagnan is arrested by the Cardinal's men.

D'Artagnan tells the Cardinal about Milady's execution. Expecting to be punished, he is shocked when the Cardinal hands him a written order promoting him to lieutenant in the Musketeers.

His fellow musketeers have other plans: Athos wants to retire, Porthos is marrying a wealthy widow, and Aramis plans to become a priest. Sad to be losing his friends all at once, D'Artagnan accepts the promotion.

The End

Alexandre Dumas was born on July 24, 1802 in Villers-Cotterêts, France, north of Paris. His father, Thomas-Alexandre Dumas, was the son of a French nobleman and a black slave who met in the French colony of Santo Domingo (now called Haiti). Back in France, Thomas-Alexandre became a general under Napoleon Bonaparte, but fell from favor with Napoleon. He died in poverty when Alexandre was only four, so Alexandre and his mother moved in with her parents, the Labourets, who ran the Hôtel de l'Épée.

Alexandre Dumas dressed as a musketeer: a caricature by André Gill (1866)

EARLY SUCCESSES

Dumas grew up in Villers-Cotterêts, spending many hours in the forest with his friends Hanniquet and Boudoux, the local poachers. He was taught by his mother and then by the village priest before becoming a clerk for a local lawyer. In 1823, aged 20, he went to Paris to find fame and fortune. Dumas got a job working for the Duc d'Orléans (later King Louis Philippe), but soon found his way into the world of theater and publishing. By 1829, he had made a name for himself with the play *Henry III and his Court*, performed by the celebrated Comédie Française, the French national theater company.

A FAMOUS PLAYWRIGHT

At first, Dumas was famous for his plays rather than for his novels. In 1832, he wrote the hugely successful play *The Tower of Nesle*. This was actually a rewrite of a work by Frédéric Gaillardet.

Gaillardet was so upset when Dumas took the credit for the rewrite that he challenged him to a duel with pistols. Luckily, neither man hit the other! Dumas wrote hundreds of plays during his lifetime, as well as travel diaries, children's stories, and a dictionary of food. He also wrote for several weekly magazines.

THE BIG SPENDER

This incredible stream of work earned Dumas over 200,000 francs a year—an enormous sum in those days. However, he lived just like the heroes of his books, spending huge sums on

extravagant parties and good living. In his lifetime he made and lost several fortunes. At 6ft 2in (1.9m) tall, he was also a man of action, taking part in the French Revolution of 1830. He caught cholera in the great epidemic of 1832, but survived.

His novels

Dumas went to Italy to recover from the disease, and there he married the actress Ida Ferrier in 1840. However, they soon broke up after he had spent all her money. Around this time, Dumas turned to writing novels, and over the next 30 years he wrote some 250 books, helped by more than 70 assistants. Because he worked on so many projects at once, Dumas color-coded his work, using blue paper for novels, yellow for plays, and pink for magazine articles!

The novels were often published as serials, with a new chapter coming out each week. Among his most famous novels are *The Three Musketeers, The Count of Monte Cristo,* and *The Vicomte of Bragelonne* (the last volume of which is often published as a separate story, called *The Man in the Iron Mask*).

Dumas' travels

By 1852, Dumas was bankrupt again and was forced to flee to Brussels, in Belgium. He returned to Paris three years later, then began a new set of adventures, traveling to England, Germany, Russia, and finally back to Italy, where he helped the republican leader Giuseppe Garibaldi during the War of Italian Unification. From 1861 to 1864 he lived in Naples, in the south of Italy, before setting off again on tours of Austria, Hungary, and Spain. In 1870, Dumas finally settled down in his son's villa in northern France, where he died on December 5.

In the family

Alexandre's son, Alexandre Dumas Jr., followed in his literary footsteps, writing many plays and several important novels, of which the most famous is *The Lady of the Camellias*. The elder Dumas is often referred to as "Dumas père" (French for "Dumas the father") to avoid confusion with his son, "Dumas fils" (Dumas the son).

Dumas' reputation

Many of Dumas' works are historical novels mixing fact with fiction. Critics accused him of distorting the truth, but his fans loved his ability to write great action stories and create larger-than-life characters. Overseas, his works were particularly popular among 19th-century African-Americans, though in public Dumas did not refer much to his African ancestry. The Scottish writer Robert Louis Stevenson—himself famous for gripping adventure stories such as *Treasure Island* and *Kidnapped*—read *The Vicomte of Bragelonne* six times and described it as his "favorite book."

Alexandre Dumas' *The Three Musketeers*, written in 1844, is the first part of a great historical epic: the author continued D'Artagnan's story in *Twenty Years After* (1845) and *The Vicomte of Bragelonne: Ten Years Later* (1850), which contains the famous story of *The Man in the Iron Mask*.

Dumas wrote these stories in short chapters: some were hammered out just a few days or even hours before they were to be printed. Despite the amazing speed at which Dumas wrote, *The Three Musketeers* instantly became popular. Long lines formed in the streets to buy newspapers carrying the latest episode.

The Three Musketeers was first published in the magazine *Le Siècle* between March and July 1844. Dumas claimed it was based on manuscripts he had discovered in the Bibliothèque Nationale (the French National Library). He certainly borrowed the names of many of the characters from *Memoirs of Monsieur d'Artagnan*, written in 1700 by Gatien de Courtilz de Sandras. Dumas borrowed these volumes from the Marseille public library in 1843 and kept them when he returned to Paris!

FACT AND FICTION

Dumas' version of the story follows D'Artagnan and his three friends from 1625 to 1628, as they get caught up in intrigues involving King Louis XIII, Cardinal Richelieu, Queen Anne, and her English lover George Villiers, First Duke of Buckingham. These are all real people, even D'Artagnan: the real-life Charles de Batz-Castelmore, Comte d'Artagnan, served in the King's

Musketeers under Louis XIII and XIV and was killed at the battle of Maastricht in the Netherlands in 1673. However, Dumas weaves historical characters and real events, such as the siege of La Rochelle, into a fantastic plot all of his own making.

KING LOUIS XIII

Louis XIII (1601–1643) was only 9 years old when his father Henry IV was assassinated. His mother ruled in his place until 1617, and in 1615 she arranged his (unhappy) marriage to Anne of Austria. With the support of Cardinal Richelieu, Louis survived countless rebellions and plots by family members. During his reign, France successfully fought against the mighty Spanish and Austrian empires during the Thirty Years' War (1618–1648). Louis often took great risks, leading his army into battle on horseback.

CARDINAL RICHELIEU

Dumas portrays Cardinal Richelieu (1585–1642) as an evil mastermind; this is a little unfair to the man who built France into a great European power.

Born Armand-Jean du Plessis, Richelieu was made Bishop of Luçon when he was only 21. In 1622 he was appointed Cardinal, and he became Louis XIII's chief minister in 1624. He was nicknamed "The Red Eminence," because cardinals wear red and their title is "Your Eminence." Richelieu packed the royal council with loyal supporters, known as his "creatures."

Portrait of Cardinal Richelieu by Philippe de Champaigne, painted about 1642

Richelieu was ruthless, but he had to be—there were at least seven plots hatched against him, some involving the King's brother Gaston and Queen Anne.

Richelieu was a skillful diplomat who made new allies for France in Germany, Holland, and Italy. He even tried to forge good relations with England by having Louis XIII's sister Henrietta Maria marry the English King Charles I. Within France, Richelieu set out to weaken the power of the nobles and the Protestant Huguenots, whom he defeated at the siege of La Rochelle.

THE DUKE OF BUCKINGHAM

In *The Three Musketeers*, Buckingham is the heroic lover of the French Queen Anne. The real George Villiers, First Duke of Buckingham (1592–1628), was a favorite of King James I of England, who made him Lord High Admiral in 1619. In 1625 he was sent to France with 600 servants to collect Princess Henrietta Maria. His arrival in Paris caused a sensation, and Queen Anne seems to have admired him.

Dashing but arrogant, Buckingham was actually more like Cardinal Richelieu in Dumas' story: hungry for power and full of madcap schemes. When he tried to arrange a marriage between the future King Charles I and a Spanish princess, the Spanish ambassador asked Parliament to have Buckingham executed. Buckingham answered by calling for a war on Spain!

In 1625 Buckingham led a disastrous attack on the Spanish port of Cádiz, which had to be called off when his troops came across a warehouse filled with wine and got hopelessly drunk.

In 1627 he launched an expedition in support of the French rebels of La Rochelle, but lost 4,000 men out of 7,000. A year later, he was preparing for another expedition when he was stabbed to death by John Felton, a survivor from the first expedition.

George Villiers, First Duke of Buckingham

THE REAL MUSKETEERS

On May 14, 1610, King Henry IV of France was stabbed to death while riding in his coach. In 1622 a new force was created to protect his successor, Louis XIII. They fought both on foot and on horseback and were armed with muskets—which earned them the name "musketeers." Although Louis was protected by his own Swiss Guards within the palace walls, whenever he went anywhere else the King's Musketeers were at his side.

SHORT BUT TOUGH!

Like D'Artagnan in the *The Three Musketeers*, many of the musketeers, including the real Captain de Tréville, came from Gascony and Béarn in southwest France—rugged mountain country known at the time for its werewolves (which were really packs of ordinary wolves). Short, tanned, and tough, the men from this region spoke a dialect that was as different from Parisian French as Spanish is. They also had a reputation for telling tall tales.

DEADLY RIVALS

A second company of musketeers was created to protect Cardinal Richelieu, and both companies were soon looking to recruit men with sword-fighting skills. Cardinal Richelieu's men were more numerous and better armed than the King's Musketeers, and this led to rivalry between the two groups. Duels were common. However, dueling was a dangerous business. Even if no one was killed, the penalty for dueling was death. When the Comte François-Henri de Montmorency-Bouteville fought several duels in the Cardinal's own palace, Richelieu had him publicly beheaded.

THE FOUR MUSKETEERS

There are, of course, four musketeers in Dumas' novel—so why is it called *The Three Musketeers*? The answer is that D'Artagnan, the main hero of the book, does not become a musketeer until near the end of the story, so for most of the time only three of the four friends are musketeers. The real-life Charles de Batz-Castelmore, Comte d'Artagnan (1611–1673) served Louis XIV as captain of the Musketeers of the Guard. He joined the Musketeers in 1632, perhaps through a family friend, Monsieur de Tréville (who was also a relation of Athos, Porthos, and Aramis).

Although in *The Three Musketeers* D'Artagnan is a rival of Cardinal Richelieu, in real life he was a spy for Richelieu's successor Cardinal Mazarin, and carried out several secret missions on behalf of King Louis XIV.

After many years of service, in 1667 D'Artagnan became captain of the Musketeers. He was killed in battle on June 25, 1673 when a musket ball ripped into his throat at the Siege of Maastricht in a war against the Dutch.

The character of Aramis was based on the real-life musketeer Henri d'Aramitz, a squire and abbot. Porthos was based upon Isaac de Portau, a musketeer and adventurer from Pau, while Athos was loosely based on the musketeer Armand de Sillègue d'Athos d'Autevielle, who was killed in a duel in 1643.

OTHER NOVELS BY DUMAS PÈRE

Here are the English titles of Dumas' most famous novels, with the dates when they were first published in French.

1838   *Captain Paul*
1844   *The Three Musketeers*
1844–1845 *The Count of Monte Cristo*
1846   *Twenty Years After*
        (sequel to *The Three Musketeers*)
1847   *Queen Margot*

1847–1850 *The Vicomte of Bragelonne*
        (second sequel to *The Three Musketeers*)
1848   *The Forty-Five Guardsmen*
1851   *The Black Tulip*
1852   *Conscience*
1853   *Taking the Bastille*
1860   *Black: The Story of a Dog*

45

Important Events

IN THE LIFETIME OF ALEXANDRE DUMAS PÈRE

1802
July 24: Dumas is born in Villers-Cotterêts, France.
French Revolutionary Wars end.

1803
Louisiana Purchase: US doubles in size after buying land from France for $15 million.

1804
Napoleon proclaims himself emperor of France.

1808
Beethoven's Fifth Symphony is first performed.

1815
Napoleon is finally defeated at Waterloo.

1819
Simón Bolívar liberates New Granada (now Colombia, Venezuela, and Ecuador) from Spain.

1822
Greece declares independence from Turkey.

1825
First passenger-carrying railway in England.

1826
Oldest surviving photograph is taken by Joseph-Nicéphore Niepce (France).

1829
Dumas becomes a leader of the Romantic movement with his play *Henry III and his Court*.

1833
Slavery is abolished in the British Empire.

1834
Charles Babbage (UK) invents the mechanical adding machine, a forerunner of computers.

1836
Boer farmers in southern Africa start the "Great Trek," founding republics in Natal, Transvaal, and Orange Free State.

1844
Samuel F. B. Morse (US) invents the telegraph.
Dumas writes *The Three Musketeers*.

1846
US declares war on Mexico (war lasts until 1849).
Failure of potato crop causes famine in Ireland.

1847
Dumas begins writing *The Vicomte of Bragelonne*.

1848
Revolutions occur across Europe. In France, Louis Napoléon is elected President of the Republic.
Karl Marx and Friedrich Engels (Germany/UK) publish the *Communist Manifesto*.

1849
Thousands rush to California in search of gold.

1851
Herman Melville (US) writes *Moby Dick*.

1853
Crimean War begins, with Russia fighting Turkey, France, and Britain (war lasts until 1856).
US Commodore Oliver Perry reaches Tokyo; Japan is forced to trade with the outside world.

1856
Gustave Flaubert (France) writes *Madame Bovary*.

1857
India becomes part of the British Empire.
First transatlantic telegraph cable.

1859
Work begins on Suez Canal (completed 1869).
Unification of Italy begins under Count Cavour.
Jean-Joseph-Étienne Lenoir (Belgium) builds the first internal combustion engine.
Charles Darwin (UK) publishes *On the Origin of Species*, setting out his theory of evolution.

1861
American Civil War begins.
Kingdom of Italy is proclaimed under Piedmontese King Victor Emmanuel II.
Louis Pasteur (France) discovers bacteria.

1865
American Civil War ends; slavery is banned.
US President Abraham Lincoln is assassinated.

1866
Alfred Nobel (Sweden) invents dynamite.
Austria is defeated by Prussia and Italy in the Seven Weeks' War.

1867
US buys Alaska from Russia for $7.2 million.

1868
Revolution in Spain.

1870
Franco-Prussian war begins (ends 1871).
December 5: Alexandre Dumas dies in Puys, near Dieppe, France.

STAGE AND SCREEN

ADAPTATIONS OF *THE THREE MUSKETEERS*

The story of *The Three Musketeers* has been made into films and adapted for TV on many occasions in the past 90 years. In 1928 the story was made into a musical, with lyrics co-written by the famous author P. G. Wodehouse, in a production that ran on Broadway for 318 performances.

The first film version was made in France in 1921: *Les Trois Mousquetaires* was a silent film starring Aimé Simon-Girard as D'Artagnan and Claude Mérelle as Milady de Winter. It was a smash hit in its day, and led to a number of sequels. In the same year, the famous actor Douglas Fairbanks Sr. starred in a Hollywood version, also a silent movie. It featured a famous stunt where Fairbanks did a one-handed handspring to grab a sword during a fight scene. For the role of D'Artagnan, Fairbanks grew a moustache—which he kept for the rest of his life.

Over the years, many alternative versions of the story have appeared on the silver screen. In 1933, the story was set in North Africa and the musketeers were members of the French Foreign Legion: John Wayne starred as D'Artagnan! The story was very popular in Russia, and a 1978 film version, *D'Artagnan and the Three Musketeers*, was set in the Soviet Union and made into a disco musical. However, a more faithful adaptation of the story on screen was made in 1973, which starred Michael York as D'Artagnan and Oliver Reed as Athos.

The *Three Musketeers* story has also inspired a number of cartoons. In 1951, Tom and Jerry starred in *The Two Mouseketeers*, which won an Oscar for best short cartoon. In the 1980s *Dogtanian and the Three Muskehounds* was a popular cartoon made by Spanish and Japanese film companies. It featured dogs as the musketeers, while the seductive Milady was a cat. In *Mickey, Donald, Goofy: The Three Musketeers* (2004), the three classic Disney characters become Royal Musketeers after rescuing the princess (Minnie Mouse) from masked bandits. In 2006, over 150 years after it was written, the story was also made into a computer game.

A colorful MGM production from 1948, with Gene Kelly as D'Artagnan

INDEX

FURTHER INFORMATION

IF YOU LIKED THIS BOOK, YOU MIGHT ALSO WANT TO TRY THESE TITLES IN THE BARRON'S *GRAPHIC CLASSIC* SERIES:

Dracula by Bram Stoker
Frankenstein by Mary Shelley
The Hunchback of Notre Dame by Victor Hugo
Journey to the Center of the Earth by Jules Verne
Kidnapped by Robert Louis Stevenson

Macbeth by William Shakespeare
The Man in the Iron Mask by Alexandre Dumas
Moby Dick by Herman Melville
Oliver Twist by Charles Dickens

FOR MORE INFORMATION ON ALEXANDRE DUMAS:

en.wikipedia.org/wiki/Alexandre_Dumas
www.kirjasto.sci.fi/adumas1.htm
www.cadytech.com/dumas